SCHEDULE

Name **Daphne Davis**

Address **2122 Lomo Drive**

School **of Disasters!**

		Period 1	Period 2	Period 3	Period 4	Period 5	Period 6	Period 7	Period 8
Time	From	50-50			not good			bad	
	To	not good			bad			worse!	
Monday	Subject			Bad Luck					
	Room								
	Instructor		Friday	the	13th				
Tuesday	Subject								
	Room		13	of	anything!				
	Instructor								
Wednesday	Subject			The	Evil Eye!				
	Room								
	Instructor								
Thursday	Subject								
	Room								
	Instructor	Being a				For more disasters			
Friday	Subject	vampire —				look for			
	Room	very bad luck!				The Name Game!			
	Instructor								

For Daphne's eyes
only!

PRIVATE!

No vampires, ghosts, or
zombies allowed!

That means YOU!

Daphne's Diary
of
Daily Disasters

by Marissa Moss

Simon & Schuster Books for Young Readers
New York   London   Toronto   Sydney

SIMON + SCHUSTER BOOKS FOR YOUNG READERS
An imprint of Simon + Schuster Children's Publishing Division
1230 Avenue of the Americas, New York, New York 10020

SIMON + SCHUSTER BOOKS FOR YOUNG READERS is a
trademark of Simon + Schuster, Inc.
For information about special discounts for bulk purchases,
please contact Simon + Schuster Special Sales
at 1-866-506-1949 or business@simonandschuster.com.
The Simon + Schuster Speakers Bureau can bring authors to
your live event. For more information or to book an event, contact the
Simon + Schuster Speakers Bureau at 1-866-248-3049 or
visit our website at www.simonspeakers.com.
Also available in a Simon + Schuster Books for Young Readers hardcover edition
A Paula Wiseman Book
Book design by Daphne (with help from Tom Daly)
The text for this book is hand-lettered.
Manufactured in China
0411 SCP
2 4 6 8 10 9 7 5 3 1
CIP Data is available from the Library of Congress
ISBN 978-1-4424-2677-1 (hc)
ISBN 978-1-4424-1737-3 (pbk)
ISBN 978-1-4424-1966-7 (eBook)

This book is dedicated to
Alexandra Penfold,
who has saved me from
many disasters!

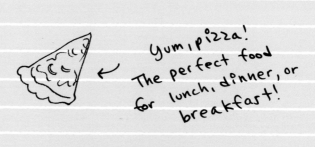

Name: Daphne Davis

Age: 9

Grade: 4th

Hometown: Oakland

Best Friend: Kaylee

Favorite Color: Pink

Hobbies: Origami and collecting cute Japanese erasers

Favorite Food: Pizza (but NOT pepperoni!)

Favorite Movie: Back to the Future (or how to avoid any disaster!)

Unfavorite Disasters —
the Worst of the Worst!

Daily Disaster, Monday

1. Mondays are always a disaster because they're the first day of the week.
2. And that's the day we run the mile, an automatic disaster for me.
3. But today it was a _worse_ disaster than usual because I tripped and fell.
4. In the mud.
5. And when I got up, I tripped AGAIN!
6. In the mud.
   Of course.
7. I ended up with muddy knees, muddy hands, muddy shoes, muddy hair (don't ask how!).
8. And my worst mile time EVER!
9. Until next Monday.

DAY ONE:

There are three really hot things in my school these days — Lamar Graham, the cutest boy in fourth grade, the horseradish the cafeteria serves with the hot dogs, and vampires. Any kind of vampire, but teenage or kid vampires are the best.

Though I imagine a vampire dog could be really cute. Or a vampire kitten.

Mew!

One of those puffball puppies would be especially adorable.

Even cuter would be a vampire hamster!

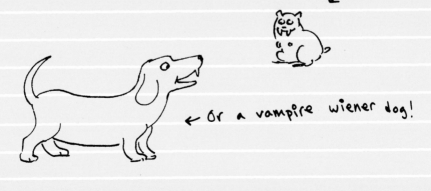

← Or a vampire wiener dog!

Lamar isn't a vampire, but he's the kind of boy who's so cute, he doesn't even know how cute he really is. Which makes him even cuter.

cute →

nice →

cute + nice =
extra, super
adorable!
superhot!

←

As for the horseradish, it's so spicy, it makes your eyes water.

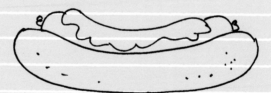

It can't make the hot dog taste good — nothing could do that — but it can burn a hole in your tongue so you don't think about how disgusting it really is. All you think is WATER NOW!!

I'm not sure why or how the vampire craze started. Maybe the horseradish sparked it. Or the nasty hot dogs. Whatever it was, vampires have definitely taken over my school. Everyone is reading vampire books.

Or talking about vampire movies.

And dressing like vampires. And by that I mean wearing those plastic fangs that normally you only see when it's Halloween. Now they're very, very popular even though it's nowhere near October.

Say blooood!

On school photo day, kids even had their pictures taken with them.

Girl vampires are hot.

Boy vampires are sizzling.

Teacher vampires are too scary — I mean REALLY scary — to be popular. They're the opposite of popular!

So when the teachers announced a costume day next Friday (again, even though Halloween is loooooooong past), I knew exactly what I wanted to dress up as:

A vampire, of course!

Kaylee, my best friend, didn't think that was such a hot idea.

"Everyone's gonna be a vampire. You'll just be one of the crowd," she said. "How dumb is that?"

"Not dumb at all," I said. "Because I'll be the <u>best</u> vampire!"

How? What does it <u>mean</u> to be the best vampire? That you have the sharpest, whitest fangs?

That's a good question and I don't have the answer. But I'm definitely going to figure it out.

vampire smiles

↓

curved, sharp, and superwhite

thick and pointy

with braces — _not_ a good thing

Kaylee wouldn't give up. She has a thing against vampires maybe just <u>because</u> they're so popular.

If you insist on being a vampire, I dare you to be the best one — better than everyone else! And I'll be something completely different.

No one will have a costume like mine!

"Oh, yeah," I said. "What are you going to be?"

"You'll see."

I could tell she wasn't going to tell me no matter what. That's an infuriating thing about Kaylee. She's good at keeping secrets. Too good. Me, I'm terrible. I can't help it — I just blurt things out.

It's like my mouth opens and says stuff all on its own — without my brain being connected to it → at all.

Did I say that?

Wasn't me! Must have been someone who looked a lot like me.

I hate it, but my brothers love that about me. They know that if they try hard enough, they can get me to tell them practically anything.

Tell us! Tell us!

What happened to the marshmallows? Spill it — NOW!

The twin glare, impossible to withstand.

Okay, I admit it! I microwaved the marshmallows. <u>All</u> of them. I started with one marshmallow PEEPS chick and I couldn't stop! I ended up with an army of giant chicks and bunnies.

giant pink, purple, and yellow blimps

David

Just as we suspected. you owe us PEEPS!

Donald

You can tell it's David by the Booger Bubble.

That kind of thing NEVER happens to Kaylee. And she's good at costumes, so I bet she comes up with something great.

Some of Kaylee's costumes from past Halloweens.
↓

a black hole
↓

Feed me! I'm hungry!

an accident waiting to happen wrapped in CAUTION tape →

punctuation →

Kids thought she was a swear word, but no, she was grammatically correct.

She's never been anything as simple or obvious as a vampire so I'm not surprised she doesn't want to be one now. Maybe if vampires weren't so popular...

Anyway, she likes clever costumes that are like nobody else's. I don't care about that — I want to be cool.

Being a vampire is my chance for a tiny trace of coolness.

But I have to figure out <u>how</u> to be a vampire and what kind to be, or I may as well be something boring and stupid like a ghost.

There's nothing cool about this at all.

Different Types of Vampires

baby vampire —
maybe wear footie
pajamas for maximum
cuteness

↙

princess vampire, for
maximum glamour

↙

↑
I'm not sure how to do
the bald head baby
curl, though.

↑
Could I wear this? Am
I princess-y enough?

nerd vampire — this
would be easier for a boy.
↙   They're
                     naturally
                     nerdier.

zombie vampire

↙

Two undead
favorites in →
one!

If I could pull off the Princess Vampire, I'd definitely choose that, but the Zombie Vampire is a safer bet. I'm great at blank stares.

I just imagine I'm listening to one of those boring health lectures in P.E. →

And right away, I look like this.

Kaylee says if I insist on being a vampire, I should be a vampire <u>bat</u>. That sounds terrible! Who wants to be a flying rodent?

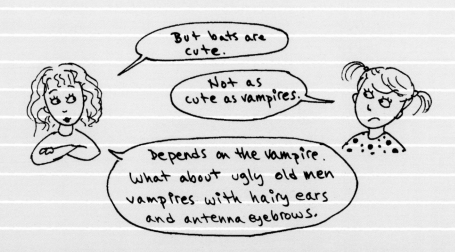

But bats are cute.

Not as cute as vampires.

Depends on the vampire. What about ugly old men vampires with hairy ears and antenna eyebrows.

Everyone knows that vampires are young – ONLY young. Because they can't die or get old and wrinkly. That's what makes them so magical. It's like they drank the Elixir of Eternal Youth – blood.

That's why it's kinda cool to get bitten by a vampire because then you'll live forever too – with no ear hairs or wiry eyebrow whiskers.

My little brothers LOVE the idea of being a vampire. But since they're in kindergarten, they aren't part of costume day. Only the older kids.

The teachers are worried that some costumes might scare the really little kids. That's why they're not included. And for the rest of us, there are some rules:

1. No terrifying rubber masks of monsters, ghouls, creatures, or anything that would give a kindergartner nightmares.

2. So no hairy gorilla heads.

3. No politician masks either— those bore people to death and THAT'S scary!

4. And NO clowns, masks or otherwise— those are freaky no matter what!

5. No weapons — rubber, paper, cardboard, or ANYTHING!

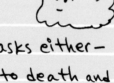

no plastic scythes →

no sporks— deadliest of all! ←

No arrows → bent over your head.

Do all these rules make the twins feel safer? No, they just think they're missing out.

"Come on, guys!" I said. "You'll get your turn next year. When you're in first grade."

I could see the lightbulb go on over Donald's head. He looked excited about something.

"But the new itty-bitty baby kindergartners won't, will they? They won't get costumes!"

"No," I agreed. "They'll have to wait, just like you."

Suddenly the twins were jumping around, happy, happy, happy.

It's true — nothing makes something as special as knowing you're getting it when other people aren't.

I'm lucky that way because I'm the oldest so I always get new privileges first. Like staying up later, a raise in my allowance, getting to do new things.

For instance, dressing up as a vampire. Whatever kind of vampire I end up picking.

I'm kind of like a scout for my younger brothers, breaking the trail for them, climbing the mountain first so they'll know which way to go.

They should appreciate me!

I asked Mom for help with my vampire costume. Since she works cutting hair at The Clip Joint, this is what she gave me.

A black smock to wear as a vampire cloak. Really, Mom, there's no resemblance ← at all, but it's black.

● ● ● ● ● ● ● ● ● ●
↑
Black press-on fingernails

White powder to make my ← face really pale like an undead person.

Black mascara and eyeliner — the best part!
Real makeup! →

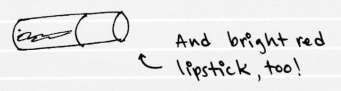

And bright red ← lipstick, too!

Me, as a Vampire
↓

I wet my hair and slicked it back to → make it look vampire-y.

I love my eyes like this! I look SO grown-up, almost ready for middle school!

The fake fingernails were a nice touch if I say so myself.

Even the smock wasn't as dorky as I thought it would be.

Black tights and black shoes to complete the Black Look.

↑
I thought I looked totally cool.

HA HA HA HA HA HA!

Donald and David didn't. They roared with laughter when they saw me. I thought they'd bust a gut. According to them, I'm a disaster as a vampire. They say I look NOTHING like one.

"Oh, yeah? Then what do I look like?" I demanded.

"A demented ghost!" Donald shrieked.

"A deranged nutcase!" David howled.

"A dingbat doo-doo-head!" they yelled together, the way only twins can. "A vampire disaster!"

"Stop it!" They really made me mad. "You're being dumb brats. Just because you're jealous that you don't get to dress up."

"Not anymore we aren't. Not if it means looking like you!" They cackled and giggled so much they were snorting out snot.

As if I cared about their opinion.

I went to my room, closed the door, and stared at the mirror on my closet.

Could the evil twins possibly be right? Was I dorky or cool?

Would I know the difference? →

Would everyone at school laugh at me like my brothers? ←

Maybe my vampire was too ordinary. I could add a tiara for a princess vampire. Or paint my cheeks green for a zombie vampire. Or draw a red line around my neck for a creepy beheaded vampire.

But would any of those things make me cool?

I gave up. I'm just not good at thinking of clever, creative ideas. Not like Kaylee.

So I called her.

"Please!" I begged. "You've got to help me figure out how to make my vampire special. I don't want to look stupid!"

"How about the vampire bat idea?"

"Kaylee!" I heard a sigh. Then silence. I waited, holding my breath.

"Okay," Kaylee said.

Hooray! I thought.

"I'll come over and we'll figure things out."

"Thank you, thank you, thank you! You're the __best__ friend ever!"

Kaylee to the rescue!

She should dress up as Super Kaylee!

"So what are you going to be for Costume Day?" I asked her as soon as I opened the front door.

"An Un-Vampire!"

"What's that?"

"Someone who's NOT a vampire," she explained, kind of.

"That's just a regular person," I said.

"Exactly!"

She looked very pleased with her logic, though I didn't get it at all. A normal person means no costume. Doesn't she want to dress up?

I mean, who doesn't want the chance to play with makeup. →

And, best of all, to pretend to be someone cool! If only I can pull it off. ←

Kaylee has different ideas.
"It's perfect! I just dress and act normally and when people ask me what I'm supposed to be, I'll tell them."

She sounded so happy with her plan, I wanted to be happy for her, even if I didn't get it.

"I guess that's clever," I said. "Or you could be a regular, normal vampire — with me. Nothing 'un' about it."

Kaylee shook her head. "The 'Un' is the best part. You go ahead and be a vampire. I'll be your opposite."

For a second, I imagined Kaylee dressing up like this:

She would look like me, → except...

... with one of those red slashes across her face that mean NO.

← Like no parking, no smoking, no food, no noise, no vampires!

But of course she wouldn't really do that. The point of her disguise (I think) is no disguise.

"Okay," I said. "You be what you want, so long as you tell me how to look like a cool vampire, not a nerdy one."

"Hmmm... are you sure? A nerdy one could be funny! Yeah, why not a nerd vampire with thick plastic glasses, a calculator on your belt, and braces on your fangs!"

I vant to suck your data!

Add pimples for maximum nerdiness!

This is my idea of a NIGHTMARE! Not a good costume at all!

"No way!" I yelled. "I want to be COOL, not UNcool! C'mon, you said you'd help me!"

"Fine! You don't have to scream!"

"I'm not, I'm just emphatic. Anyway you haven't said a word about how I look. What do you think?"

Kaylee circled around me, staring up and down and all over. I could tell she was thinking because her forehead was scrunched up.

Kaylee's concentration lines — she calls them brain waves.

Hmmm . . .

"You definitely need something," she finally said. "I just have to figure out what."

She didn't have much of a chance to think because Donald and David came running in from the backyard, making lots of noise and tracking in mud.

Mom hates it when they do this — footprints and handprints everywhere!

"Eek!" Donald shrieked. Or maybe it was David. I couldn't see which one had the Booger Bubble. "It's a terrible vampire!"

"Terribly boring, you mean!" David scoffed. Or maybe it was Donald.

"You're right," Kaylee said. "Daphne needs some oomph, some pizzazz, some oomphazz! Any ideas?"

The twins were thrilled that anybody cared about their opinion. I sure didn't. I glared at Kaylee, but she ignored me.

"Don't ask them! They don't know what's cool!" I snapped.

"Yes, we do!" they shouted.

"I don't want kindergarten cool! I want fourth grade cool!" Because everyone knows kindergarten cool = fourth grade dork.

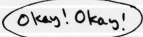

Kaylee held out her arms like she was a referee → at a soccer game.

Okay! Okay!

But that didn't calm down the twins. No surprise since they never listen to <u>real</u> referees.

The boys started spinning around like human tops, trying to drive me crazy. I hate when they get like this — like SUPER-WILD MANIACS!

I grabbed Kaylee's wrist and we escaped to my room. Good thing the door locks. I could hear my brothers pounding on the door.

"We're zombies! We're going to eat you!"

"GO AWAY!"

They pounded some more, but then they got bored and went away.

"See what I have to put up with?" I was still sore at Kaylee. She should never have encouraged them. It's best to ignore them.

"Too bad you're not a real vampire," Kaylee said. "Then you could freeze them with one glare of your vampire-y eyes."

"Vampires can't do that. Anyway forget about them. Make _me_ cool!"

This is what Kaylee did.

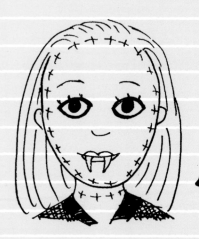

She drew stitches with eyebrow pencil around my face and neck.

"Why?" I asked. "Am I a rag-doll vampire?"

"No, I'm not sure why. But they make you more interesting."

"Are you sure?" I stared in the mirror. I guessed it was an improvement. Maybe.

"You look great!" Kaylee sounded absolutely, positively sure.

So I believed her.
BIG mistake! HUGE!
Because that's how I dressed for Costume Day, only it turned out that no one thought I looked cool.
Just the opposite.

She has cooties!

Don't touch her!

She's contagious!

Stay away from Daphne!

She's a walking disaster

It was the worst day of my life. And it was all Kaylee's fault. My best friend's fault! I was miserable and furious at the same time (which is actually kind of tricky).

Kaylee made a bunch of lame-o excuses, but none of them mattered because I had just sunk to the bottom of the social scale in fourth grade. Now no one was lower than me. Not even the kid with the weird skin disease and superthick glasses.

Everyone, EVERYONE was cooler than me!

I was crushed at the bottom of the pyramid.

How long would I be stuck on the bottom, like gum on a shoe? How would I crawl my way back to somewhere near the middle? Or at least <u>one</u> layer above the bottom?

Being the lowest of the low meant nobody would walk home with me or sit with me at lunch. Well, Kaylee would. But only Kaylee, nobody else.

And who would ever invite me to their birthday parties or give me a valentine?

The rest of the year looked pretty bleak. Me, pariah for all of fourth grade.

Here's what I imagined for tomorrow, and the next day and the next.

↓

Nothing ↙   ↙ and more nothing

↑

as far as the eye could see.

I thought dressing like a vampire would make me MORE popular, not less. Now I just want to be a ghost and disappear.

Turns out this would have been a much better costume.

Who knew? How do the cool kids guess what will be cool? And why do I get it so wrong?

Kaylee tried to cheer me up but I was so mad at her, I didn't want to be near her. I know I might have been a vampire disaster even without her help, but I blamed her anyway.

GRRRRRRe

GRRRRRRR

All I could do was growl at her.
I swear last period took forever. The
minutes crawled by.

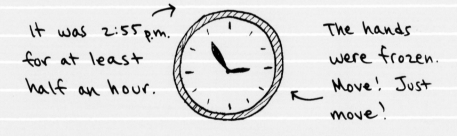

It was 2:55 p.m.
for at least
half an hour.

The hands
were frozen.
Move! Just
move!

School clocks are never right anyway,
but today was the worst EVER!

BRRRRRRRRRNGG!

At last, I could escape all the stares and
teasing. I ran all the way home.

Mom could tell something was wrong as soon as I got there.

"What happened in Vampire Land?" she asked.

"It was a total disaster!" I wailed.

I raced to my room to change, to scrub my face, to turn back into myself.

Here's what I saw. →

← Who knew that plain old me could be such an improvement?

My brothers must have heard me.

What happened? What happened? What went wrong?

Donald and David actually looked worried, so I told them the whole, ugly truth.

"Wow, that's bad," said one.
"Really bad," said the other.
  They're only kindergartners and they got it — that was a superbad sign of how bad my life was now.

  I screamed and cried and threw the stuffed animals on my bed. The twins stared at me, but they didn't leave. They watched until I wore myself out.

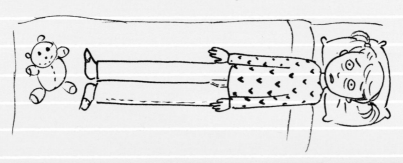

David whispered something to Donald. Donald grinned and whispered something back.

"Okay, what is it?" I demanded. "No secrets allowed in my room. Unless they're mine."

We have an idea!

A great idea!

of how to get rid of your vampire cooties forever!

"How?" I asked. Could they really know?

"You have to transfer them," David said.

"To someone — or some<u>thing</u> — else," Donald explained. "Something else has to have the cooties, and we know what it should be!"

They ran out of my room and came back with a broken doll, something that looked like it should have been thrown away a long time ago.

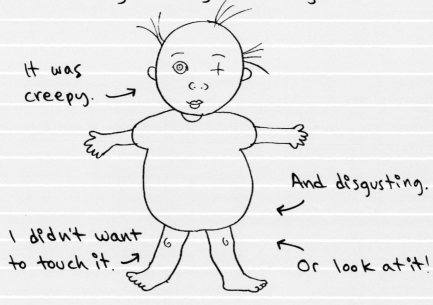

It was creepy. →

And disgusting.
←

I didn't want to touch it. ↗

← Or look at it!

"It's the perfect cootie catcher!" David said.
   "It's already full of cooties!" added Donald.
   They had a point. If anything had cooties, that doll did!
   "But how do I get my cooties onto the doll? How do I add cooties to more cooties?"

The twins gave each other the twin look. It's like a secret signal they have. Then Donald whispered into my right ear. And David whispered into my left ear.

I smiled.
It could work—it really could.
I have to admit, my brothers are pretty smart, even if they're only in kindergarten. Maybe because they're in kindergarten. After all, kids that age are EXPERTS at cooties!
So the next day I took the doll to school (wrapped in a plastic bag so I wouldn't have to touch it), and put the plan into action.

I started with Kaylee. I whispered into her ear.

Pssssshhh

She whispered into Georgia's.

Pssssshhh

Pssssshhh

Georgia whispered into Emma's.

And soon the whole fourth grade was talking about it.

Of course, when things are whispered like that, words get changed.
"I ate a tuna sandwich for lunch"
  becomes
"I made the wrong kind of hunch"
  which becomes
"I made the basketball crunch"
  which becomes
"Barbecue is tasty for brunch"
  which becomes
"Blisters are better to munch."
None of which make much sense.
   So what I said to Kaylee at the beginning of the day got changed in all sorts of ways, but the important part stayed the same. All the rumors had the same absolutely essential word:

   cootie.
   Some heard cootie catcher. Others heard cootie hatcher. Others still heard cootie snatcher, latcher, and scratcher.

But along the way somebody heard enough to make them want to look in the girls' bathroom by the cafeteria.

I knew when it happened because you could hear the scream all the way out by the tetherball poles.

And in the special, saved-for-only-kindergartners playground, Donald and David gave each other that twin look again, I'm sure of it.

So that's how the Super Creepy Cootie Story got started in our school. No one dared to touch the doll. No girl will ever use that bathroom again.

And with everybody busy talking about the Super Creepy Cootie Spot, my cooties were boring, old news, nowhere near as exciting.

The next day at school I checked, but the janitor must have thrown out the doll. It didn't matter. The cooties were still there. That bathroom stayed jinxed.

And I was a normal nobody once again. Not cool, but not full of cooties anymore, either.

what do cooties look like anyway?

Some kind of bug? Or germ?

who knows?

So I'm not mad at Kaylee. She's not mad at me. It's all regular fourth-grade stuff again.

Except it's like there's a magnetic field around that girls' bathroom. No one goes even close to that door. →

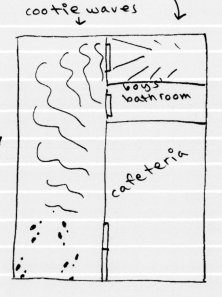

cootie bathroom

cootie waves ↓

↓

boys' bathroom

cafeteria

Donald and David were very proud of themselves. They saved me, PLUS they made their mark on school — a very big mark. They were so excited, they told Mom and Dad the whole story.

Mom was not pleased, but Dad thought the whole thing was hilarious.

Maybe, but I still have to finish fourth grade, and there's lots I need to learn. Even if I never do figure out how to be cool. At least I've learned how to escape the cootie trap.

And how **not** to be a vampire.

This diary
better STAY
private!!

DAPHNE ONLY
allowed access!

Disaster Doodles

Dorky Vampires
(dorkier than me!)
↓

kitty vampire

pig vampire

duckling vampire

chicken vampire

basset hound vampire

Costume Disasters

Forgetting to wear a costume at all, and making a lame-o excuse when people ask you what you're supposed to be.

Wearing a costume that's a hand-me-down and doesn't fit.

Putting together a last-minute costume from stuff around the house.

Kaylee, you always have such great ideas for costumes. Have you ever had a costume disaster?

Of course! Nobody's perfect, not even me.

So what was it?

It was a long time ago, before I met you. It was Halloween. I wanted to be something really scary, the scariest thing I could think of.

But you don't like scary costumes! You never have!

Usually I don't. But this once I wanted to try being something different, something scary.

So what were you?

you know me - I couldn't be anything ordinary like a monster or a vampire. So I decided to be the most terrifying thing I could think of - an overflowing toilet! But there was no way to make that costume.

What did you end up doing?

I just put a plunger in my belt and said I was Joe the Plumber. I ended up not being scary at all.

I dunno. A plumber sounds pretty creepy to me.

It was a disaster!

Disaster Doodles

costume falls off

costume too heavy to wear for long

Disaster Doodles

costume that stinks-
literally!

costume that looks like
a _different_ costume

Disaster Doodles

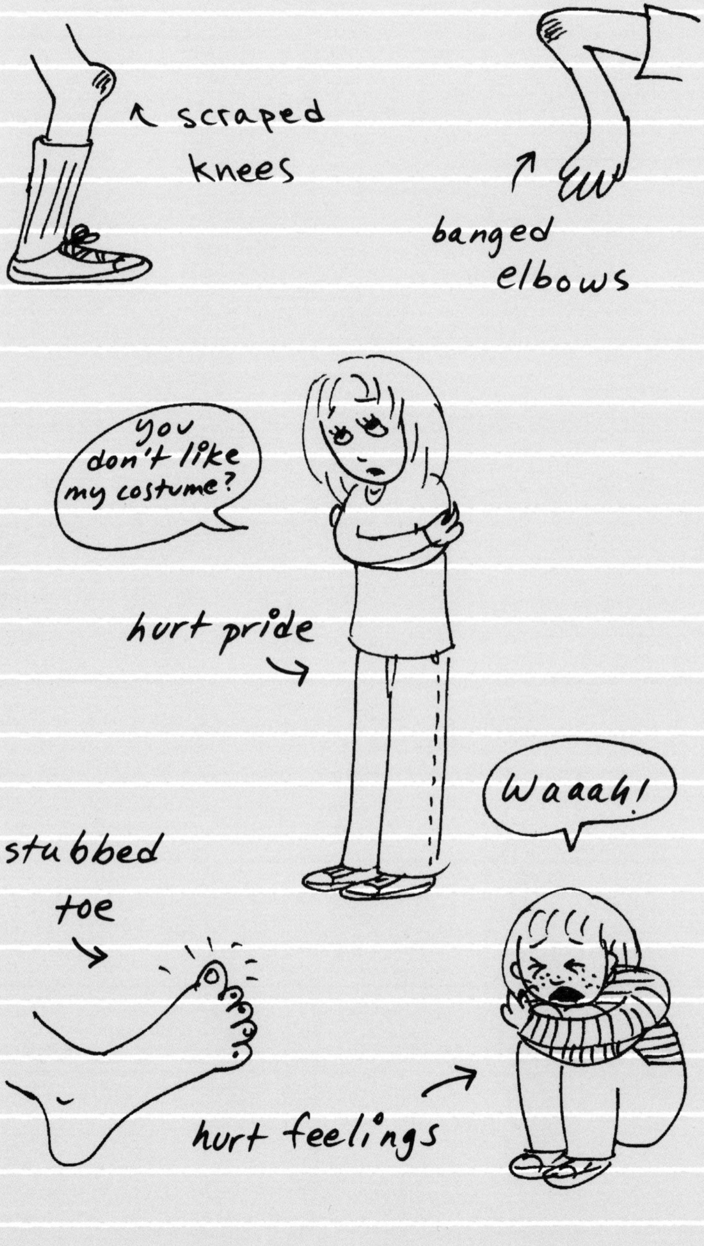

Disaster Doodles

↓

↑
headache from
so many disasters

↑
eyeache from
sneaking peeks
in someone else's
diary

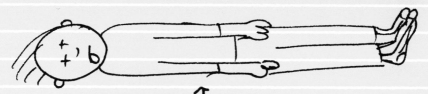

everywhereache — ↑ just leave me alone!

Unfavorite Disasters—
the Worst of the Worst!

Daily Disaster, Friday
1. Friday is supposed to be a good day because there's no school tomorrow.
2. But not today.
3. Because there was a pop quiz in math.
4. Which I hadn't studied for, of course, because it was a pop quiz.
5. And I think I did bad, I mean really, really bad.
6. Which is really, truly, SUPER bad because when we were done, the teacher said it would count for a lot of our grade.
7. Happy weekend!

What's the worst way to start
the weekend?

With stomach flu?

With tons of homework?

With an annoying chore?

What's the worst thing you
can fall into?

mud?

shark-infested waters?

a bottomless pit?

wavy lines stand for major stinkiness

overflowing toilet ooze?

Cafeteria Menu
advance warning of what NOT to eat!

Monday
Baked Fish Fillet on Wheat Bun
Baked Spicy Chicken on Wheat Bun
Turkey Pepperoni Pizza

Tuesday
Macaroni & Cheese
Turkey Hot Dog on Wheat Bun
Bagel & Cream Cheese

Wednesday
Golden Trout Treasures ←
BBQ Beef on Wheat Bun
Peanut Butter & Jelly Sandwich

They have to call it a treasure because no way would anybody eat it otherwise.

Thursday
Spaghetti & Garlic Bread
Beef & Bean Burrito
Peanut Butter & Jelly Sandwich

↑ They tried plain Golden Trout but it sounded like cat food.

Friday
Chicken Teriyaki on Brown Rice
Cheese Quesadilla
Turkey Corn Dog on Wheat Bun

↑ Choose stomachache, big burps, or major farting — that's the real menu!

Diary Doodles of Hot Stuff

↓

↑
cocoa

fire↗

↑
chips and salsa

And NOT Hot Stuff
↓

↑
plain white
socks

↑
Swiss
cheese

↑
paperclips
and rubber bands

If you haven't had enough disaster, there's more!

Daphne's Diary of Daily Disasters

And for yet more disastrous stuff, go to marissamoss.com.